Sophie Johnson: unicorn expert

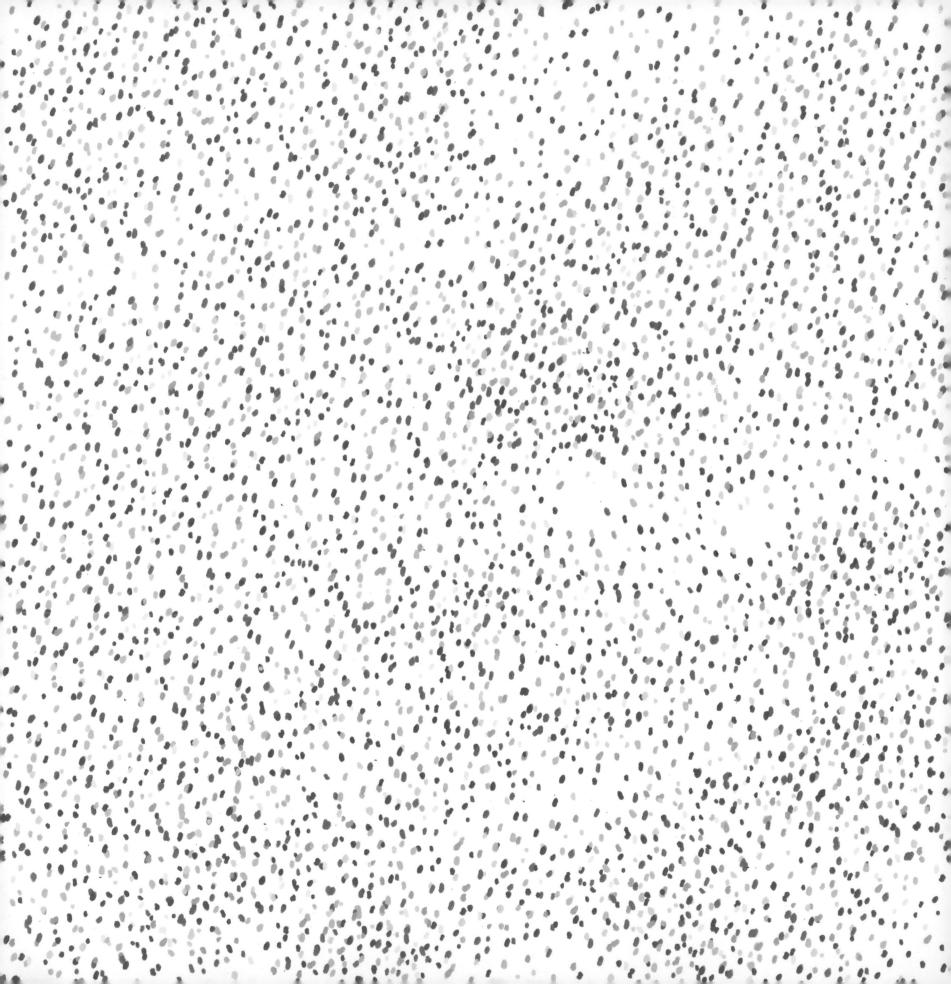

For Anna and Flora - MH

To my family: SE, HC, PA, OJ - EO

SIMON & SCHUSTER

First published in Great Britain in 2018 by Simon & Schuster UK Ltd • 1st Floor, 222 Gray's Inn Road, London, WC1X 8HB • A CBS Company • Text copyright © 2018 Morag Hood • Illustrations copyright © 2018 Ella Okstad • The right of Morag Hood and Ella Okstad to be identified as the author and illustrator of this work has been asserted by them in accordance with the Copyright, Designs and Patents Act, 1988 • All rights reserved, including the right of reproduction in whole or in part in any form • A CIP catalogue record for this book is available from the British Library upon request.

978-1-4711-4561-2 (HB) • 978-1-4711-4562-9 (PB) • 978-1-4711-4563-6 (eBook)

Printed in China • 10 9 8 7 6 5 4 3 2 1

Sophie Johnson: unicörn expert

Morag Hood and Ella Okstad

SIMON & SCHUSTER
London   New York   Sydney   Toronto   New Delhi

My name is
Sophie Johnson
and I live with
a **unicorn**.

Well, not just one actually.

I think I have **17** at the moment.

It can be hard work looking after so many.

There is always a lot to do.

Luckily, I am a unicorn expert.

I am very busy teaching my unicorns everything they need to know.

We start with **MAGIC.**

Then I show them how to hunt for food . . .

. . . and I teach them
about the dangers of . . .

BALLOONS!

Sometimes my unicorns
lose their horns.

But I don't worry,

because they soon grow back.

Living with unicorns can be a bit tricky.

They are quite messy.

I try to explain that magic
is more important than mess,

but I don't think Mum understands.

Unicorns have many enemies,

so sometimes,

I **have** to protect them.

Being a unicorn expert
is harder than you'd think.

Really, it's a good job I'm here.

Some people don't even know what a **REAL** unicorn looks like!

That's why they need me -
Sophie Johnson, Unicorn Expert.

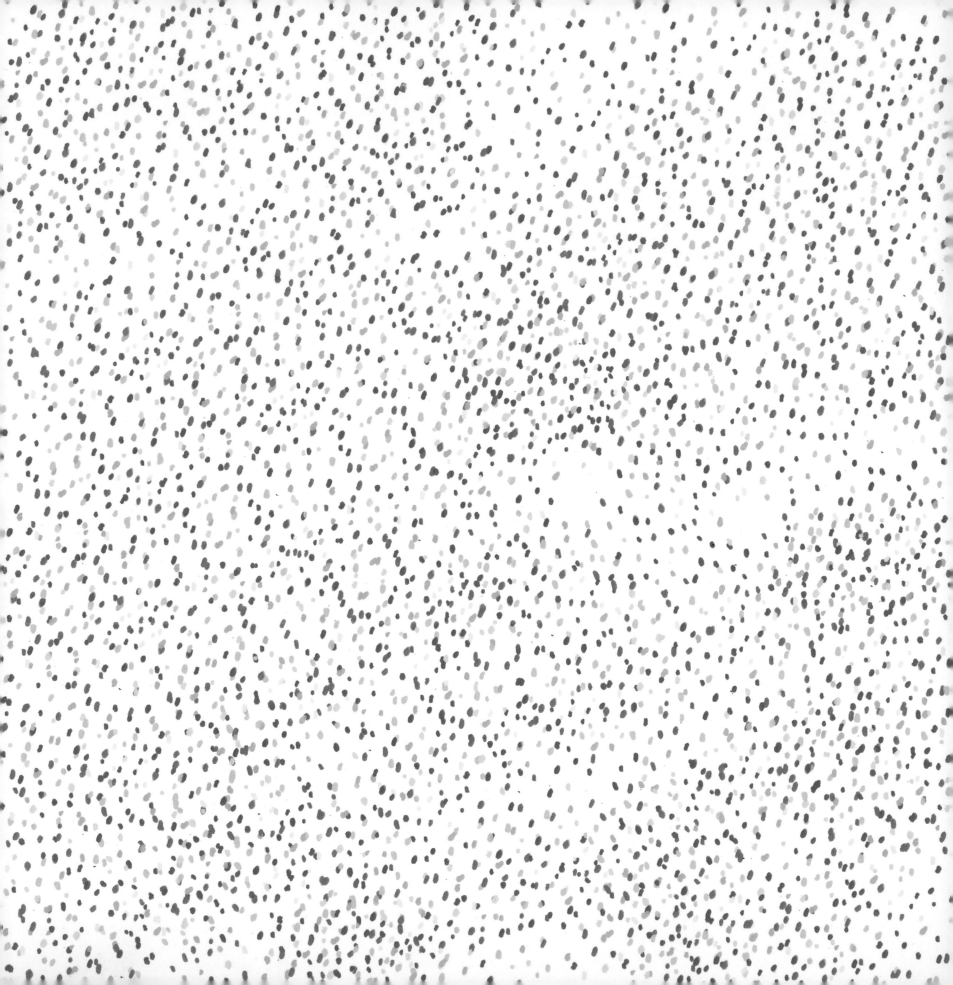

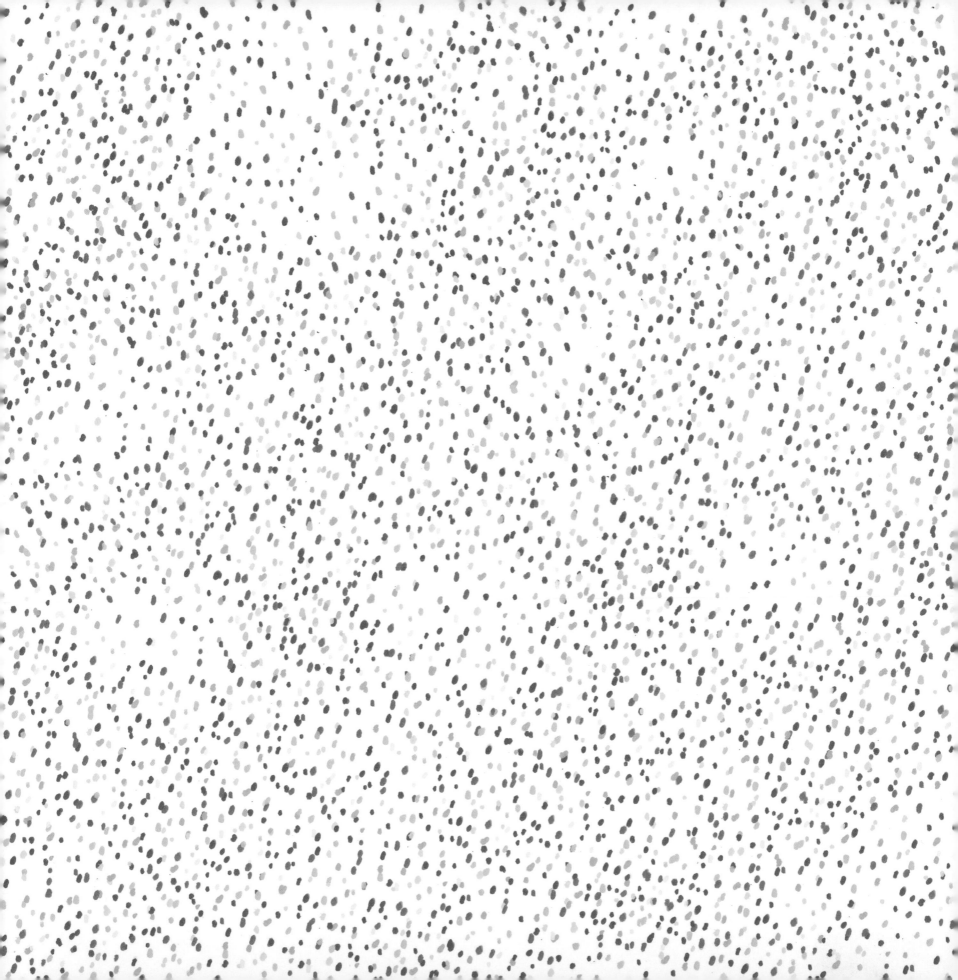